weetzie
bat

Also by Francesca Lia Block

weetzie bat

Francesca Lia Block

A CHARLOTTE ZOLOTOW BOOK
HarperCollins*Publishers*

Library of Congress Cataloging-in-Publication Data
Block, Francesca Lia
  Weetzie Bat.

  "A Charlotte Zolotow book."
  Summary: Follows the adventures of Weetzie Bat and her Los Angeles
friends, Dirk, Duck, and My Secret Agent Lover Man.
  [1. Friendship—Fiction. 2. Los Angeles (Calif.)—Fiction.] I. Title.
PZ7.B61945We   1989   [Fic]   88-6214
  ISBN 0-06-020534-2
  ISBN 0-06-020536-9 (lib. bdg.)
  ISBN 0-06-440818-3 (pbk.)

Typography by Alicia Mikles

Tenth anniversary edition, 1999

For my father, Irving Alexander Block

contents

weetzie
bat

Weetzie
and Dirk

THE REASON WEETZIE BAT hated high school was because no one understood. They didn't even realize where they were living. They didn't care that Marilyn's prints were practically in their backyard at Graumann's; that you could buy tomahawks and plastic palm tree wallets at Farmer's Market, and the wildest, cheapest cheese and bean and hot dog and pastrami burritos at Oki Dogs; that the waitresses wore skates at the Jetson-style Tiny Naylor's; that there was a fountain that turned tropical soda-pop colors, and a canyon where Jim Morrison and Houdini used to live, and all-night potato knishes at

Canter's, and not too far away was Venice, with columns, and canals, even, like the real Venice but maybe cooler because of the surfers. There was no one who cared. Until Dirk.

Dirk was the best-looking guy at school. He wore his hair in a shoe-polish-black Mohawk and he drove a red '55 Pontiac. All the girls were infatuated with Dirk; he wouldn't pay any attention to them. But on the first day of the semester, Dirk saw Weetzie in his art class. She was a skinny girl with a bleach-blonde flat-top. Under the pink Harlequin sunglasses, strawberry lipstick, earrings dangling charms, and sugar-frosted eye shadow she was really almost beautiful. Sometimes she wore Levi's with white-suede fringe sewn down the legs and a feathered Indian headdress, sometimes old fifties' taffeta dresses covered with poetry written in glitter, or dresses made of kids' sheets printed with pink piglets or Disney characters.

"That's a great outfit," Dirk said. Weetzie was wearing her feathered headdress and her moccasins and a pink fringed mini dress.

"Thanks. I made it," she said, snapping her strawberry bubble gum. "I'm into Indians," she said. "They were here first and we treated them like shit."

"Yeah," Dirk said, touching his Mohawk. He smiled. "You want to go to a movie tonight? There's a Jayne Mansfield film festival. *The Girl Can't Help It.*"

"Oh, I love that movie!" Weetzie said in her scratchiest voice.

Weetzie and Dirk saw *The Girl Can't Help It*, and Weetzie practiced walking like Jayne Mansfield and making siren noises all the way to the car.

"This really is the most slinkster-cool car I have ever seen!" she said.

"His name's Jerry," Dirk said, beaming. "Because he reminds me of Jerry Lewis. I think Jerry likes you. Let's go out in him again."

Weetzie and Dirk went to shows at the Starwood, the Whiskey, the Vex, and Cathay de Grande. They drank beers or bright-colored canned Club drinks in Jerry and told each other how cool they were. Then they went into the clubs dressed to kill in sunglasses and leather, jewels and skeletons, rosaries and fur and silver. They held on like waltzers and plunged in slamming around the pit below the stage. Weetzie spat on any skinhead who was too rough, but she always got away with it by batting her eyelashes and blowing a bubble with her gum. Sometimes Dirk dove offstage into the crowd. Weetzie hated that, but of course everyone always caught him because, with his black leather and Mohawk and arm-loads of chain and his dark-smudged eyes,

Dirk was the coolest. After the shows, sweaty and shaky, they went to Oki Dogs for a burrito.

In the daytime, they went to matinees on Hollywood Boulevard, had strawberry sundaes with marshmallow topping at Schwab's, or went to the beach. Dirk taught Weetzie to surf. It was her lifelong dream to surf—along with playing the drums in front of a stadium of adoring fans while wearing gorgeous pajamas. Dirk and Weetzie got tan and ate cheese-and-avocado sandwiches on whole-wheat bread and slept on the beach. Sometimes they skated on the boardwalk. Slinkster Dog went with them wherever they went.

When they were tired or needed comforting, Dirk and Weetzie and Slinkster Dog went to Dirk's Grandma Fifi's cottage, where Dirk had lived since his parents died. Grandma Fifi was a sweet, powdery old lady who baked tiny, white, sugar-coated pastries for them, played them tunes on a music box with a little dancing monkey on top, had two canaries she sang to, and had hair Weetzie envied—perfect white hair that sometimes had lovely blue or pink tints. Grandma Fifi had Dirk and Weetzie bring her groceries, show her their new clothes, and answer the same questions over and over again. They felt very safe and close in Fifi's cottage.

"You're my best friend in the whole world," Dirk said to Weetzie one night. They were sitting in Jerry drinking Club coladas with Slinkster Dog curled up between them.

"You're my best friend in the whole world," Weetzie said to Dirk.

Slinkster Dog's stomach gurgled with pleasure. He was very happy, because Weetzie was so happy now and her new friend Dirk let him ride in Jerry as long as he didn't pee, and they gave him pizza pie for dinner instead of that weird meat that Weetzie's mom, Brandy-Lynn, tried to dish out when he was left at home.

One night, Weetzie and Dirk and Slinkster Dog were driving down Sunset in Jerry on their way to the Odyssey. Weetzie was leaning out the window holding Rubber Chicken by his long, red toe. The breeze was filling Rubber Chicken so that he blew up like a fat, pocked balloon.

At the stoplight, a long, black limo pulled up next to Jerry. The driver leaned out and looked at Rubber Chicken.

"That is one bald-looking chicken!"

The driver threw something into the car and it landed on Weetzie's lap. She screamed.

"What is it?" Dirk exclaimed.

A hairy, black thing was perched on Weetzie's knees.

"It's a hairpiece for that bald eagle

you've got there. Belonged to Burt Reynolds," the driver said, and he drove off.

Weetzie put the toupee on Rubber Chicken. Really, it looked quite nice. It made Rubber Chicken look just like the lead singer of a heavy-metal band. Dirk and Weetzie wondered how they could have let him go bald for so long.

"Weetzie, I have something to tell you," Dirk said.

"What?"

"I have to wait till we get to the Odyssey."

At the Odyssey, Weetzie and Dirk bought a pack of cigarettes and two Cokes. Dirk poured rum from the little bottle he kept in his jacket pocket into the Cokes. They sat next to the d.j. booth watching the Lanka girls in spandy-wear dancing around.

"What were you going to tell me?" Weetzie asked.

"I'm gay," Dirk said.

"Who, what, when, where, how—well, not how," Weetzie said. "It doesn't matter one bit, honey-honey," she said, giving him a hug.

Dirk took a swig of his drink. "But you know I'll always love you the best and think you are a beautiful, sexy girl," he said.

"Now we can Duck hunt together," Weetzie said, taking his hand.

Duck
Hunting

THERE WERE MANY KINDS of Ducks—
Buff Ducks, Skinny Ducks, Surf
Ducks, Punk-Rock Ducks, Wild
Ducks, Shy Ducks, Fierce Ducks, Cuddly
Ducks, Sleek, Chic G.Q. Ducks, Rockabilly
Ducks with creepers and ducktails, Rasta
Ducks with dreads, Dancing Ducks, and
Skate-Date Ducks, Ducks in Duckmobiles
racing around the city.

Weetzie and Dirk went to find the Ducks
of their respective dreams.

At a gig at Cathay de Grande, Weetzie
stood in front of the stage feeling Buzz's sweat
flinging off him as he sang. He was bald, with

tattoos all over his arms. Weetzie stared up into the lights.

"That is no Duck," Dirk said. "That is one wild vulture bird."

"But he is gorgeous, isn't he?" Weetzie said, watching Buzz's nostrils flare.

She was pretty drunk by the end of the gig. Buzz came out from backstage and grabbed her wrists.

"How was I?" he asked.

"You were okay." Weetzie swallowed.

"Okay? I was hot."

"You think you are pretty sexy, don't you?"

"Yes. So are you. Come and get a beer with me."

He turned and backed Weetzie up against the wall. She smelled leather and beer.

"Put your arms around my neck."

She did it, pretending to choke him, and he pulled her up onto his glossy, white back.

"Put me down!"

She tried to kick him with her engineer boots but he carried her toward the bar.

After he had let her down, he felt the pockets of his Levi's for change.

"Shit." He turned to Weetzie. "Let's go to my place. I got some beers."

He looked about twelve suddenly, even with the shaved head, the eyeliner, and the skull earring.

Weetzie started to walk away.

"Come on," he said softly.

Weetzie clung to Buzz's body as they rode his motorcycle through the night. Wind blew on their faces, a summer wind thick with the smell of all-night taco stands.

Buzz lived in the basement of an old house. The walls were covered with graffiti for his band, Head of Skin, and there was a mattress in one corner. Weetzie glimpsed the handcuffs for a second before Buzz had her down on the mattress. She kept her eyes on the bare bulb until it blinded her.

In the morning, Weetzie tried to wake Buzz but he grunted when she touched him and pulled the sheets over his head. She got out of bed, wincing, still drunk, and called Dirk. He came and picked her up outside.

"Are you okay?" she asked him. His eyes were red. He had met someone in a video booth at a local sex store and they had groped around there for a while, then gone to the guy's apartment. Dirk had awakened, looked at the unfamiliar face, and gone home fast.

"About the same as you, I think."

They went to Canter's for bagels, which comforted Weetzie because she had teethed on Canter's bagels when she was a baby. While they ate, a cart of pickles wheeled by, the green rubbery pickles bobbing.

"Oh, God, that's all I need to see after last night," Dirk said.

"There are no Ducks, it feels like," Weetzie said.

"What is that?" Dirk asked the next day, noticing a tattoo-like bruise on Weetzie's arm.

"Nothing," she said.

"You aren't seeing that Buzz vulture anymore," Dirk said.

Weetzie kept falling for the wrong Ducks.

She met a Gloom-Doom Duck Poet who said, "My heart is a canker sore. I cringed at the syringe."

She met a toothy blonde Surf Duck, who, she learned later, was sleeping with everyone.

She met an Alcoholic Art Duck with a ponytail, who talked constantly about his girlfriend who had died. Dirk saw him at an all-boy party kissing all the boys.

Dirk didn't do much better at the parties or bars.

"I just want My Secret Agent Lover Man," Weetzie said to Dirk.

"Love is a dangerous angel," Dirk said.

Weetzie and Her Dad at the Tick Tock Tea Room

WEETZIE'S DAD, CHARLIE BAT, took her to the Tick Tock Tea Room. "We're the only people here without white hair . . . well, naturally white," Weetzie's dad said. Weetzie's hair was bleached white.

Weetzie's dad ordered two turkey platters with mashed potatoes, gravy, and cranberry sauce. The white-haired waitress served them canned fruit cocktail, sugar-glazed rolls, and pink sherbet before the turkey came. They had apple pie afterward.

"Does your mother feed you?" Weetzie's dad asked between the fruit and the rolls. "You're wasting away."

"Dad!" Weetzie said. "Of course she does."

"And how is your mother?"

"She's okay. Why don't you come in and see her later?"

"No, thanks, Weetzie. Not a good idea. But say hello from me," he said wistfully. "Any boyfriends? You, I mean."

"No, Dad."

"What about that Dirk? Still seeing him?"

"Yeah, but we're just friends."

Weetzie smiled at her dad. He was so handsome, but he didn't look well. He reminded her of a cigarette.

"I wish you'd come in and say hi to Mom," Weetzie said when Charlie dropped her off. But she knew that Charlie and Brandy-Lynn still weren't speaking.

Charlie came to L.A. from Brooklyn in the late fifties. He wrote to his older sister, Goldy, "Here I am in the L.A. wasteland. I hate the palm trees. They look like stupid birds. Everyone lies around in the sun like dead fishes. I go back to my little hotel room and my sad bed and feel sorry for myself. Saving all my pennies. Still no work. But I keep hoping."

Charlie got a job as a special-effects man at the studios. Making cities and then making them crumble, creating monsters and wounds and rains and planets in space. But what he really wanted to do was to write screenplays. He finished *Planet of the Mummy Men* and showed it to a producer, Irv Finegold.

"I like it, I like it," Irv said. They were having martinis at the Formosa. "And I'd like to make it."

Brandy-Lynn was a starlet who got a role in *Mummy Men*. She was on the set, having a fight with the director because she thought the mummy rags were unflattering, when Charlie saw her.

"Love at first sight, I swear," he would say later. "The most beautiful woman I'd ever seen."

She was bleach-blonde and sparkling with fake jewels, although she was wrapped in bandages. He wrote a new part into the movie for her so she didn't have to dress like a mummy.

"He made me feel like crying the first time I saw him," Brandy-Lynn told Weetzie with a sigh. "How right I was!" she added cynically.

They made love in the heat in Brandy-Lynn's bungalow, the filmy white drapes blowing with an occasional desert breeze. They drank tequila sunrises and bathed in gin. "That was your father's idea." They drove to the beach and made love in a tent under a pink-flamingo sky. They drove down the strip in Charlie's pale-yellow T-bird, Brandy-Lynn kicking her feet—in their gold mules with the fake fruit over the toes—right out the window.

When Weetzie was born Charlie said, "Best accident I ever had." (He had crashed the T-bird twice, because Brandy-Lynn was distracting him with kisses.)

"Where did you get a name like Weetzie Bat?" Dirk had asked when they met.

"Weetzie, Weetzie, Weetzie," she had shrilled. "How do I know? Crazy parents, I guess."

"I'll say."

She wished that the romance between Charlie and Brandy-Lynn had lasted.

But Brandy-Lynn turned bitter, that's what Weetzie's dad said. "Bitter as . . . what's the bitterest thing, Weetz?"

And Brandy-Lynn said, "That man was

incorrigible. Chasing women. A real lush. And who knows what other substances he was abusing." She downed her cocktail and patted the corners of her mouth with a cherry-printed napkin held in tanned and polished fingers. "I need a Valium."

They had screamed and thrown glasses at each other in the heat. One night, Weetzie saw them by the luminous blue condo pool; Brandy-Lynn threw a drink in Charlie's face. "That's it," he said.

Charlie moved back to New York to write plays. "Real quality stuff. This Hollywood trash is bullshit."

He sent Weetzie postcards with pictures of the Empire State Building or reproductions of paintings from the Metropolitan Museum, Statue of Liberty key chains, and plastic heart jewelry. He wanted Weetzie to move back east but Brandy-Lynn wouldn't hear of it. And although Weetzie adored her father, who reminded her of a cigarette, of Valentino, of a prince with palm trees on his shoulders, she couldn't leave where it was hot and cool, glam and slam, rich and trashy, devils and angels, Los Angeles.

"Okay, baby, so you can come visit me, at least."

When she visited him, he took her to the Metropolitan and to the Museum of Modern Art, took her to Bloomingdale's and bought her perfume and shoes, rode with her on the Staten Island ferry, took her to the delis for pastrami sandwiches and Cel-Ray tonic, bought her hot pretzels on the street.

One night when they got back, the power had gone out in Charlie's apartment building and they had to walk up nine flights in the dark carrying the lox and bagels and cream cheese and bon-bons. He sang to her the whole way.

"Rag Mop. R-a-g-g M-o-p-p. Rag Mop dood-
ley-doo."

When Weetzie left, she cried into his
tobacco jacket. But really she couldn't live in
New York, where the subways made her nerves
feel like a charm bracelet of plastic skeletons
jangling on a chain. She wished that Charlie
would move back to L.A.

Instead, he came to visit and took her to
the Tick Tock Tea Room. And he asked about
Brandy-Lynn. But he never came into the
house.

Fifi's Genie

ONE DAY, WEETZIE AND DIRK brought Grandma Fifi tomatoes from the Fairfax market and prune pastries from Canter's. As they were leaving, Fifi called them back.

"You look sad," she said.

"We want Ducks," Dirk said.

Fifi looked them up and down. Then she pointed to her canaries in their cage.

"They are in love. But even before they were in love they knew they were going to be happy and in love someday. They trusted. They have always loved themselves. They would never hurt themselves," Fifi said.

Dirk looked at Weetzie. Weetzie looked at Dirk.

"I have a present for you, Miss Weetzie Bat," Grandma Fifi said.

She went to the closet and brought out the most beautiful thing. It was a golden thing, and she put it into Weetzie's hands. Then she kissed Weetzie's cheek.

As Weetzie and Dirk left Fifi's cottage, Weetzie looked back and saw Fifi standing on the porch waving to them. She looked paler and smaller and more beautiful than Weetzie had ever seen her.

When she got home, Weetzie set the thing on her table and looked at it. Despite the layers of dust she could see the exotic curve of its belly and the underlying gleam.

"I'll just polish you up," Weetzie said.

So Weetzie took out a rag and began to polish the thing.

But before she knew it, steam or smoke started seeping out from under the lid. A wisp of white vapor that smelled like musty cupboards and incense poured out and began to take shape there in the room.

Slinkster Dog whined and Weetzie gasped as they saw a form emerging. Yes, it was more and more solid. Weetzie could see him—it was a man, a little man in a turban, with a jewel in his nose, harem pants, and curly-toed slippers.

"Lanky lizards!" Weetzie exclaimed.

"Greetings," said the man in an odd voice, a rich, dark purr.

"Oh, shit!" Weetzie said.

"I beg your pardon? Is that your wish?"

"No! Sorry, you just freaked me out."

"I am the genie of the lamp, and I am here to grant you three wishes," the man said.

Weetzie began to laugh, maybe a little hysterically.

"Really, I don't see what is so amusing," the genie sniffed.

"Never mind. Okay. I wish for world peace," Weetzie said.

"I'm sorry," the genie said. "I can't grant that wish. It's out of my league. Besides, one of your world leaders would screw it up immediately."

"Okay," Weetzie said. "Then I wish for an infinite number of wishes!" As a kid she had vowed to wish for wishes if she ever encountered a genie or a fairy or one of those things. Those people in fairy tales never thought of that.

"People in fairy tales wish for that all the time," the genie said. "They aren't stupid. It just isn't in the records because I can't grant that type of wish."

"Well," Weetzie said, a little perturbed, "if this is my trip I think at least you could *say* I could have one of these wishes come true!"

"You get three wishes," the genie said.

"I wish for a Duck for Dirk, and My Secret Agent Lover Man for me, and a beautiful little house for us to live in happily ever after."

"Your wishes are granted. Mostly," said the genie. "And now I must be off."

"Don't you want to go back into your lamp?" Weetzie asked.

"Certainly not!" the genie said. "I've done my duty. I owed Fifi one more set of wishes, and she used them up on you. I'm not going back into that dark, smelly, cramped lamp. Farewell."

The genie was gone in a puff of smelly smoke.

"What a trip!" Weetzie said. "I'd better call Dirk. I wonder if someone put something in my drink last night."

Before Weetzie could call Dirk, the phone rang.

"I have good news and bad news," Dirk said. "Which first?"

"Bad," Weetzie said.

"My Grandma Fifi died," Dirk said.

"Oh, Dirk." Weetzie felt her heart stealing all the blood in her body.

"We knew she wasn't going to live very long," Dirk said.

"I know, but I never really thought she was going to die! That's a whole different thing," Weetzie said. The only death she had known was a dog named Hildegard that had belonged to Charlie Bat. The dog was the same tobacco color as Charlie and followed him everywhere, walking with the same loping stride. When Hildegard died, Weetzie saw Charlie cry for the first time.

"But, Weetz, there is good news. I feel a

little guilty about good news but I know Fifi would be really happy."

"What?"

"She left us her house!" Dirk said.

"Oh, my God!" Weetzie said.

"What's wrong?"

Fifi's house was a Hollywood cottage with one of those fairy-tale roofs that look like someone has spilled silly sand. There were roses and lemon trees in the garden and two bedrooms inside the house—one painted rose and the other aqua. The house was filled with plaster Jesus statues, glass butterfly ash-trays, paintings of clowns, and many kinds of coasters. Weetzie and Dirk had always loved the house.

Weetzie felt terrible about her wish, but Dirk said, "You didn't wish for that house or to get it that way. And she was sick anyway.

And she wanted us to have the house. She even wanted you to have her dresses. She told me that a million times."

"I don't know," Weetzie said, chewing her fingernails with their Egyptian decals.

"Now, look at these dresses," Dirk said, opening the closet.

Weetzie had never seen such great dresses—a black dress with huge silk roses sewn on it, a cream chiffon dress embroidered with gold sequins, a gold lamé and lace coat, a white fox fur, a tight red taffeta dress.

"Lanky lizards." Weetzie sighed. "They are so beautiful."

"She's lucky she had you, because I know she wouldn't want them to go to a stranger. And I know she secretly wished that I was a girl, but you serve the same purpose."

"Oh, Grandma Fifi, thank you," Weetzie said.

Duck

"I MET THE BEST ONE!" Dirk said. "The perfect Duck. But what is so weird is that this Duck calls himself Duck. Now that is hell of weird!"

"Lanky lizards!" Weetzie said.

"What now?"

Weetzie could not believe how wild it was.

Duck was a small, blonde surfer. He had freckles on his nose and wore his hair in a flat-top. Duck had a light-blue VW bug and he drove it to the beach every day. Sometimes he slept on picnic tables at the beach so he could be up at dawn for the most radical waves.

Dirk met Duck at Rage. Duck was standing alone at the bar when Dirk came up and offered to buy him a beer. Duck looked up at Dirk's chiseled features, blue eyes, and grand Mohawk. Dirk looked down at Duck's freckled nose and blonde flat-top. The flat-top was so perfect you could serve drinks on it. It was love at first sight. They danced the way some boys dance together—a little awkward and shy at first but with a sturdy ease, a rhythm between them. Dirk's heart was pounding. He didn't even feel like finishing his drink.

He imagined the feel of Duck's skin—still warm and salty from the afternoon sun. Duck grinned and looked down at his feet in their white Vans. His teeth and his Vans glowed in the dark. His long eyelashes looked so soft on his tan cheek, Dirk thought.

"I haven't asked anyone home in a long

time," Dirk said. "And we don't have to do anything. I don't know. . . ."

"I'd love to," Duck said solemnly, looking straight at Dirk.

Weetzie was happy that they had their house. She was happy that Dirk had a Duck. Duck moved in with Dirk—into the blue bedroom. Weetzie had the pink one. They were a threesome. A foursome if you counted Slinkster Dog. They went surfing together, dancing together. They all sat together on Jerry's front seat. They had barbecues and ate hamburgers and watermelon. They were a threesome all day (a foursome with Slinkster Dog included).

At night, Dirk and Duck kissed Weetzie on the cheek and went to bed. Weetzie got into her bed with Slinkster Dog. Sometimes she heard muffled giggles and love noise through the walls. Sometimes she heard music drowning out any sounds.

Weetzie couldn't help wondering why the third wish hadn't come true.

Jah-Love

WEETZIE WAS WORKING AS a waitress at Duke's. One day a tall Rastafarian man, a tiny Chinese woman with black hair tipped in orange and red like a bouquet of bird of paradise, and a baby with skin the dusty brown of powdered Hershey's hot-chocolate mix came in for breakfast. The family came in often, and pretty soon Weetzie became friends with them. The man's name was Valentine Jah-Love and the woman's name was Ping Chong. They had met in Jamaica while Ping was looking for new ideas for her spring fashion line. She had gone to Valentine's house in the rain forest to see the fabrics he silkscreened, when suddenly the sky cracked and rain poured down.

"Jah!" cried Valentine, lifting his stormy face up in the greenish electric light. "You'll have to stay here. It will rain for seven days and seven nights."

It rained and rained. The house smelled moist and muddy. Valentine carved huge Rasta-man heads, animals, and pregnant women out of wood. The second night, Ping got out of the bed she had been sleeping in and got into the cot beside Valentine. They slept together every night after that until the rain stopped on the seventh night. In the morning, Ping took an armload of fabrics silkscreened with snakes and birds, suns and shells, and went out into the steamy hot hibiscus air of Jamaica. After she had flown back to L.A., Ping found that she was pregnant. She wrote to

Valentine and said, "I am having your child. If you ever want to see us you can find us here."

Valentine came to L.A. with an old leather bag full of fabrics and carvings. He arrived at the door of Ping's Hollywood bungalow looking like an ebony lion. He said he had come to live with her.

The child they had was a boy named Raphael Chong Jah-Love. They all lived together and wore red and ate plantain and black beans, or wonton soup and fortune cookies, and made silkscreened clothing they sold on the boardwalk at Venice beach. Weetzie loved Valentine and Ping and Raphael. They took her to the Kingston 12 to hear reggae music and drink Red Stripe Jamaican beer and they gave her sarong mini skirts and turbans they made and told her about Jamaica.

"In Jamaica there is night life like nowhere else—your body feels radiant, like orange lights, like Bob Marley's voice, when you dance in the clubs there. In Jamaica we climb the falls holding hands and the water rushes down bluer than your eyes. In Jamaica. In Jamaica it is hot and wet, and the people are hot and wet, and the shells look like flowers, and the flowers look like shells, and when you drive down some roads men come out of the bushes wearing parrots on their shoulders and flowering bird cages on top of their heads."

Weetzie said, "Maybe in Jamaica I could find My Secret Agent Lover Man. I can't seem to find him here." At night she dreamed of purple flowers and babies growing on bushes.

One day she was driving Valentine and Ping and Raphael to the L.A. airport to fly to Jamaica for a few weeks. Driving south on La Cienega, past the chic restaurants and galleries, down by the industrial oil-field train-track area, was a wall with graffiti that said,

"Jah Love."

"Jah Love," Valentine said. "See that. Jah Love. That is a sign."

"Jah Love," Weetzie said wistfully.

"You need a man," Ping said. "But just you wait. I know you'll find your Jah-Love man."

"Coffee, black," he said.

It was a Sunday morning at Duke's.

"Anything else?" Weetzie asked.

"I'd like to put you in my film. My Secret Agent Lover Man." He put out his hand to shake.

"What?" Weetzie's eyes widened. She had been mistaken for a boy before and was a little sensitive about it. All she needed now was some gay man trying to pick up on her!

"My Secret Agent Lover Man's my name."

Weetzie was relieved that he hadn't been calling her *his* Secret Agent Lover Man, and that My Secret Agent Lover Man was . . .

"Your name!" she shrieked.

"Yeah. I know it's a little weird."

"Dirk put you up to this."

"Who's Dirk?"

"Lanky lizards!" Weetzie said, sitting down at the booth, knees buckling. "No way! I mean this is the wildest!"

"I know my name's weird but that's no reason not to give me a chance," he said.

A man at the next table was grumbling.

"I've got to go," Weetzie said.

My Secret Agent Lover Man came every day to see Weetzie. He was her height and wore a slouchy hat and a trench coat. He was unshaven and had the greenest eyes Weetzie had ever seen.

"I really want you to be in my film," My Secret Agent Lover Man said. "It's about a girl who comes to L.A. to be a filmmaker, and she's always taking home movies of everything, and by accident she gets some footage of a guy, and she goes around searching for him because he's the man of her dreams. She has to search in all these places like the Hollywood Wax Museum and Graumann's Chinese and Farmer's Market and Al's Bar. It's all black and white and dim and eerie and beautiful. And then at the end you realize a guy who is obsessed with the *girl* has been filming *her* all along."

My Secret Agent Lover Man took out his home-movie camera and started to shoot Weetzie in her waitress apron while she stood waiting for his order. She put her hand over the lens. She had always wanted to be a star, and, yes, he looked like her Secret Agent Lover Man, but she was afraid to believe this was real. She couldn't handle another disappointing Duck.

"Sorry, mister," Weetzie said.

"Then at least let me take you out for a drink after work."

"Some drink after work!" Weetzie said.

My Secret Agent Lover Man had driven her to the beach on the back of his motorcycle and pulled a bottle of pink champagne out of his trench coat. They were sitting on the sand by the sea. My Secret Agent Lover Man uncorked the champagne and handed the bottle to Weetzie. He got out his camera and filmed her taking a swig.

"I said no film!" Weetzie said, scowling into the camera.

"That's beautiful!" he said.

Weetzie splashed champagne at the camera lens, but My Secret Agent Lover Man kept filming.

Suddenly, the tide came in. It came up

over them, spilling over Weetzie's skinny legs, spilling over My Secret Agent Lover Man's legs in the slouchy trousers.

"Lanky lizards!" Weetzie shrieked.

My Secret Agent Lover Man laughed and laughed and kept filming her.

"Stop it!" Weetzie shouted, trying to grab the camera away.

My Secret Agent Lover Man took her wrists in his hands. Weetzie and My Secret Agent Lover Man sat there covered with salt water staring at each other. Weetzie had never noticed how pretty My Secret Agent Lover Man's lips were.

He kissed her.

A kiss about apple pie à la mode with the vanilla creaminess melting in the pie heat. A kiss about chocolate, when you haven't eaten chocolate in a year. A kiss about palm trees speeding by, trailing pink clouds when you drive down the Strip sizzling with champagne. A kiss about spotlights fanning the sky and the swollen sea spilling like tears all over your legs.

And there were a lot more of those kisses after that. On the motorcycle, in the restrooms of nightclubs, in the bathtub, in the pink bedroom. In between kisses My Secret Agent Lover Man made films of Weetzie putting her hands and feet into the movie-star prints at Graumann's, serving French toast at Duke's, dressing up in Fifi's gowns, roller-skating down the Venice boardwalk with Slinkster Dog pulling her along, Weetzie having a pow-wow and taking bubblebaths. Sometimes he filmed her surfing with Dirk and Duck, or doing a reggae dance with Ping while Valentine and Raphael played drums.

"My Secret Agent Lover Man is very cute and cool," Dirk told Weetzie.

"*Your* Secret Agent Lover Man?"

"No, I mean *your* Secret Agent Lover Man. Where did he get such a weird name?"

Weetzie just smiled beneath her feathered headdress.

And so Weetzie and My Secret Agent Lover Man and Dirk and Duck and Slinkster Dog and Fifi's canaries lived happily ever after in their silly-sand-topped house in the land of skating hamburgers and flying toupees and Jah-Love blonde Indians.

Weetzie Wants a Baby

"WHAT DOES 'HAPPILY EVER AFTER' mean anyway, Dirk?" Weetzie said. She was thinking about buildings. The Jetson-style Tiny Naylor's with the roller-skating waitresses had been torn down. In its place was a record-video store, a pizza place, a cookie place, a Wendy's, and a Penguin's Yogurt. Across the street, the old Poseur, where Weetzie and Dirk had bought kilts, was a beauty salon. They had written their names on the columns of the porch but all the graffiti had been painted over. Even Elvis Land was gone. Elvis Land had been in the front yard of an old house on Melrose. There had been a beat-up pink Cadillac, a picture of Elvis, and a giant love letter to Elvis on the lawn.

Then there were the really old places. Like the Tiki restaurant in the Valley, which had gone out of business years ago and had become overgrown with reeds so that the Tiki totems peered out of the watery-sounding darkness. Now it was gone—turned into one of the restaurants that lined Ventura Boulevard with valets in red jackets sitting out in the heat all day waiting for BMW's. And Kiddie Land, the amusement park where Weetzie's dad, Charlie, had taken her (Weetzie's pony had just dawdled, and sometimes turned around and gone back to the start, because Weetzie wouldn't use the whip, and once Weetzie was traumatized by a plastic cow that swung onto the track); Kiddie Land was now the big, brown Beverly Center that Weetzie would have painted almost any other color—at least, if they *had* to go ahead and put it up in place of Kiddie Land.

"What does happily ever after mean anyway?" Weetzie said.

She was still living in Fifi's cottage with Dirk and Duck and My Secret Agent Lover Man. They had finished their third film, called *Coyote*, with Weetzie as a rancher's daughter who falls in love with a young Indian named Coyote and ends up helping him defend his land against her father and the rest of the town. They had filmed *Coyote* on an Indian reservation in New Mexico. Weetzie grew her hair out, and she wore Levi's and snaky cowboy boots and turquoise. Dirk and Duck played her angry brothers; Valentine did the music, and Ping was wardrobe. My Secret Agent Lover Man was the director. His friend Coyote played Coyote.

The film was quite a success, and it brought Weetzie and My Secret Agent Lover Man and Dirk and Duck and their friends money for the first time. They bought a mint 1965 T-bird, and Weetzie went to Gräu and bought a jacket made out of peach and rose and gold silk antique kimonos. They had enough to go to Noshi for sushi whenever they wanted (which was a lot because Weetzie was addicted to the hamachi, which only cost $1.50 an order). They also ate guacamole tostadas at El Coyote (which had, they agreed, some of the best decorations in Hollywood, especially the painting with the real little lights right in it), putting the toppings of guacamole, canned vegetables, Thousand Island dressing, and cheese into the corn tortillas that were served between two plates to keep them warm. Weetzie also bought beads and feathers and white Christmas lights and roses that she saved and dried. She decorated everything in sight with these things until the whole house was a collage of glitter and petals.

"I feel like Cinderella," Weetzie said, driving around in the T-bird, wearing her kimono jacket, while My Secret Agent Lover Man covered her with kisses, and Dirk and Duck and Slinkster Dog crooned along with the radio.

Everything was fine except that Weetzie wanted a baby.

"How could you want one?" My Secret Agent Lover Man said. "There are way too many babies. And diseases. And nuclear accidents. And crazy psychos. We can't have a baby," he said.

They had hiked to the Hollywood sign and were eating canned smoked oysters and drinking red wine from real glasses that My Secret Agent Lover Man had packed in newspaper in his backpack.

"But we could have such a cool, beautiful baby," Weetzie said, sticking her toothpick into an oyster. "And it would be so happy and we would love it so much."

"I don't want one, Weetz," he said. "Just forget about babies—you have enough already anyway: me and Dirk and Duck and Slinkster Dog. And you're just one yourself."

Weetzie stood up, shoved her hands into the back pockets of her Levi's, and looked out over the top of the Hollywood sign. My Secret Agent Lover Man and Weetzie had spray-painted their initials on the back of the "D" when they first met. Beneath the sign the city was only lights, safe and sparkling, like the Hollywood in "Hollywood in Miniature" on Hollywood Boulevard. It didn't look like any of the things that My Secret Agent Lover Man was talking about.

The next day, My Secret Agent Lover Man

came home carrying a cardboard box that made scratching, yipping sounds. "I brought you a baby," he said to Weetzie. "This is Go-Go Girl. She is a girlfriend for Slinkster Dog. When she grows up, she and Slink can have some more babies for you. We can have as many puppy babies as you want."

Slinkster Dog wriggled with joy, and Weetzie kissed My Secret Agent Lover Man and held Go-Go Girl against her chest. The puppy's fur had a pinkish cast from her skin and she wore a rhinestone collar. She would make a perfect girlfriend for Slinkster Dog, Weetzie thought. But she was not a *real* baby.

"We'll have a baby with you," Dirk said.

He and Duck had come home to find Weetzie alone on the living room couch among the collage pillows, which were always leaving a dust of glitter and dried petals. She was crying and blowing her nose with pink Kleenex, and there were wadded up Kleenex roses all over the floor.

"Yeah," Duck said. "I saw it on that talk show once. These two gay guys and their best friend all slept together so no one would know for sure whose baby it was. And then they had this really cool little girl and they all raised her, and it was so cool, and when someone in the audience said, 'What sexual preference do you hope she has?' they all go together, they go 'Happiness.' Isn't that cool?"

"But what about My Secret Agent Lover Man?" Weetzie said.

"Nothing has to change," Dirk said. "We'll just have a baby."

"But he doesn't want one."

"It might not be his baby," Dirk said. "But I'll bet he likes it when he sees it, and we'll all go to a doctor to make sure we can make the perfect healthy baby."

Weetzie looked at Dirk's chiseled features and Duck's glossy, tan, surfer-dude face and she smiled. It would be a beautiful slinkster girl baby, or a hipster baby boy, and they would all love it more than any of their parents had ever loved them—more than any baby had ever been loved, Weetzie thought.

When My Secret Agent Lover Man came home that night he looked weary. His eyes looked like glasses of gin. Weetzie ran to kiss him, and when she put her arms around him, he felt tense and somehow smaller.

"What's wrong, honey-honey?"

"I wish I could stop listening to the news," he said.

Weetzie kissed him and ran her hands through his hair.

"Let's take a bath," she said.

They lit candles and incense, and made Kahlua and milks, and got into the bathtub in the pink-and-aqua-tiled bathroom. Weetzie felt as if she were turning into steam and milk and honey. She massaged My Secret Agent Lover Man's pale, clenched back with aloe vera oil and pikake lotion.

"If I was ever going to have a baby, it would be with you, Miss Weetzie," he said after they had made love. "You would make a great mom."

Weetzie just kissed his fingers and his throat, but she didn't say anything about the plan.

One night, while My Secret Agent Lover Man was away fishing with his friend Coyote, Weetzie and Dirk and Duck went out to celebrate. They had received their test results, and now they could have a baby. At Noshi, they ordered hamachi, anago, maguro, ebi, tako, kappa maki, and Kirin beer. They were buzzing from the beer and from the burning neon-green wasabe and the pink ginger and from the massive protein dose of sushi. ("Like, sushi is the heavy protein buzz," Duck said.)

"Here's to our baby," Dirk said. "I always wanted one, and I thought I could never get one, and now we are going to. And it will be all of ours—My (your) Secret Agent Lover Man's, too."

They drank a toast and then they all got into Dirk's car, Jerry, and drove home.

Weetzie changed into her lace negligée from Trashy Lingerie and went into Dirk and Duck's room and climbed into bed between Dirk and Duck. They all just sat there, bolt upright, listening to "I Wanna Hold Your Hand."

"I feel weird," Weetzie said.

"Me too," Dirk said.

Duck scratched his head.

"But we want a baby and we love each other," Weetzie said.

"I love you, Weetz. I love you, Dirk," Duck said.

"'I Wanna Hold Your Hand,'" the Beatles said.

And that was how Weetzie and Dirk and Duck made the baby—well, at least that was how it began, and no one could be sure if that was really the night, but that comes later on.

When My Secret Agent Lover Man came back from fishing with Coyote he looked healthier and rested. "I haven't seen the paper in three weeks," he said, sitting down at the kitchen table with the *Times*.

Weetzie took the paper away. "Honey, I have something to tell you," she said.

Weetzie was pregnant. She felt like a

Christmas package. Like a cat full of kittens. Like an Easter basket of pastel chocolate-malt eggs and solid-milk-chocolate bunnies, and yellow daffodils and dollhouse-sized jelly-bean eggs.

But My Secret Agent Lover Man stared at her in shock and anger. "You did what?

"The world's a mess," My Secret Agent Lover Man said. "And there is no way I feel okay about bringing a kid into it. And for you to go and sleep with Dirk and Duck without even telling me is the worst thing you have ever done."

Weetzie could not even cry and make Kleenex roses. She remembered the day her father, Charlie, had driven away in the smashed yellow T-bird, leaving her mother Brandy-Lynn clutching her flowered robe with one hand and an empty glass in the other, and leaving Weetzie holding her arms crossed over her chest that was taking its time to develop into anything. But My Secret Agent Lover Man was not going to send Weetzie postcards of the Empire State Building, or come visit every so often to buy her turkey platters at the Tick Tock Tea Room like Charlie did. Weetzie knew by his eyes that he was going away forever. His eyes that had always been like lakes full of fishes, or waves of love, or bathtub steam and candle smoke, or at least like glasses of gin when he was sad, were now like two heavy green marbles, like the eyes of the mechanical fortune-teller on the Santa Monica pier. She hardly recognized him because she knew he didn't recognize her, not at all. Once, on a bus in New York, she had seen the man of her dreams. She was twelve and he was carrying a guitar case and roses wrapped in green paper, and there were raindrops on the roses and on his hair, and he hadn't looked at her once. He was sitting directly across from her and staring ahead and he didn't see anyone, anything there. He didn't see Weetzie even though she had known then that someday they must have babies and bring each other roses and write songs together and be rock stars. Her heart had felt as meager as her twelve-year-old chest, as if it had shriveled up because this man didn't recognize her. That was nothing compared to how her heart felt when she saw My Secret Agent Lover Man's dead marble fortune-teller eyes.

Nine months is not very long when you consider that a whole person with fingers and toes and everything is being made. But for Weetzie nine months felt like a long time to wait. It felt especially long because she was not only waiting for the baby with its fingers and toes and features that would reveal who its dad was, but she was also waiting for My Secret Agent Lover Man, even though she knew he was not going to come.

Dirk and Duck were wonderful fathers-in-waiting. Dirk read his favorite books and comic books out loud to Weetzie's stomach, and Duck made sure she ate only health food. ("None of those gnarly grease-burgers and NO OKI DOGS!" Duck said.) They cuddled with her and gave her backrubs, and tickled her when she was sad, to make sure she got enough physical affection. ("Because I heard that rats shrivel up and die if they aren't, like, able to hang out with other rats," Duck said.) Whenever Weetzie thought of My Secret Agent Lover Man and started to cry, Dirk and Duck waited patiently, hugged her, and took her to a movie on Hollywood Boulevard or for a Macro-Erotic at I Love Jucy. Valentine and Ping and Raphael came over with fortune cookies, and pictures and poems that Raphael had made. Brandy-Lynn called and said, "I don't approve . . . but what can I get for you? I'm sure it's a girl. She'll need the right clothes. None of those feathered outfits."

Weetzie was comforted by Dirk and Duck, Valentine, Ping, Raphael, and even Brandy-Lynn, and by the baby she felt rippling inside of her like a mermaid. But the movie camera and the slouchy hat and baggy trousers and the crackly voice and the hands that soothed the jangling of her charm-bracelet nerves—all that was gone. My Secret Agent Lover Man was gone.

Weetzie had the baby at the Kaiser on Sunset Boulevard, where she had been born.

"Am I glad that's over!" Duck said, coming into Weetzie's hospital room with a pale face. "Dirk has been having labor pains out there in the waiting room."

"What about you?" Dirk said to Duck. "Duck has been moaning and sweating out there in the waiting room."

Weetzie laughed weakly. "Look what we got," she said.

It was a really little baby—almost too little.

"You can't tell who it looks like yet," Duck said. "It's too little and pink."

"No matter who it looks like, it's all of ours," Dirk said. He put his arms around Weetzie and Duck, and they sat looking at their baby girl.

"What are we going to name it?" Duck said.

They had thought about Sweet and Fifi and Duckling and Hamachi and Teddi and Lambie, but they decided to name her Cherokee.

When they left the hospital the next day, Weetzie looked down Sunset Boulevard to where Norm's coffee shop used to be. Weetzie's dad, Charlie, had waited all night in that Norm's, drinking coffee black and smoking packs until Weetzie was born. Weetzie had always thought that when she had a baby its father would wait in Norm's for her, looking like her secret agent lover. But Norm's was torn down and My Secret Agent Lover Man was gone.

Weetzie and Dirk and Duck brought Cherokee home and the house felt different, lighter and more musical now, because someone was always opening a window to let in the sun or putting on a record. The sun streamed in, making the walls glow like the inside of a rose. But even in the rosy house, Weetzie felt bittersweet; bittersweetness was like a liqueur burning in her throat and dripping down slowly into her heart.

Then one morning, Weetzie woke up feeling different, not bittersweet, but expectant the way she used to feel on the morning of her birthday. She opened her eyes and saw the flowers—there were flowers heaped on top of the quilt. Big, ruffly peonies, full-blown roses, pink-spotted lilies, pollen-dusty poppies. Weetzie blinked in the sunlight and saw My Secret Agent Lover Man standing over her and Cherokee. He looked very pale and hunched in his trench coat, and his eyes were moist.

Weetzie put out her arms, and he came and sat on the bed and held her very tight. Then he looked at Cherokee.

"Whose is she?" he asked. "She is so completely perfect."

"She looks like Dirk," Weetzie said. "Because of her cheekbones."

My Secret Agent Lover Man's mouth twitched a little.

"And she looks like Duck," Weetzie said. "Because she is blonde . . . And her nose."

My Secret Agent Lover Man wrinkled his brow.

"And she looks like me, of course, because she is so itsy-witsy and silly-looking," Weetzie said, laughing.

"But really, she absolutely has no one else's eyes but yours, and your pretty lips. I think she's all of ours," Weetzie said. "I hope that is okay with you."

Dirk and Duck came into the room.

"We missed you," Dirk said. "And we hope you stay around and help raise our kid."

My Secret Agent Lover Man smiled. Weetzie held Cherokee against her breast. Cherokee looked like a three-dad baby, like a peach, like a tiny moccasin, like a girl love-warrior who would grow up to wear feathers and run swift and silent through the L.A. canyons.

Witch Baby

ONE DAY, THERE WAS a knock on the door of the silly-sand-topped house. Weetzie opened the door, and there stood a beautiful woman with long black hair, purple, tilty eyes, and a long body. She was the type of woman Weetzie and Dirk used to call a "Lanka."

"Is Max here?" asked the Lanka in a low voice.

"Who?" Weetzie said. It came out like a screech, especially compared to the Lanka murmur, and she said again, "Who?"

"Max," the woman repeated. "I know he lives here. I've tracked him down."

"There is no one by that name here,"

Weetzie said. "I'm sorry I can't help you."

"I insist on seeing Max," the woman said, pressing on Weetzie's chest with five taloned fingertips.

Weetzie pushed the Lanka away and shut the door.

"Curses on both of you!" the Lanka said.

Weetzie looked out the peephole and saw her slink away down the front path in her long, black Lanka dress.

At dinner that night, Weetzie said, "A crazy woman was here today. She kept asking for some man. She was a real Lanka—a mean Lanka, too. It was a little scary."

"There are a lot of freaks around," Dirk said.

"Yeah," Duck said. "Next time something like that happens, call us."

"I can handle it," Weetzie said.

My Secret Agent Lover Man was unusually silent.

The next night, My Secret Agent Lover Man came home early from the set where he had been working on his new horror movie about a coven of witches who pose under the guise of a Jayne Mansfield fan club. His skin was burning and he looked as if there was a heavy weight pressing on his forehead and his shoulders. Weetzie put him in bed and took his temperature, which was very high. She gave him aspirin and megadoses of vitamin C and sponged him off with cool towels.

"You have been working too hard," she said.

My Secret Agent Lover Man gasped for air all through the night. Weetzie lay awake, watching him so hot and vulnerable, shivering with fever, and she wanted to hold on to him and never let go. It was as if he had no defenses, none of his usual guards up, as if they could merge together so easily.

"I love you, Weetzie," he said in the middle of the night. Then he twisted as if from a sharp pain.

"I love you, I love you, My Secret Agent Lover Man, my wish list come true," she said.

In the morning, he was still sick. Weetzie brought him more aspirin and vitamin C, and made him drink grapefruit juice and herb tea, and she put on cartoons for him to watch.

"I have to tell you something, Weetzie," he said.

"Not now; try to rest. I'm taking you to the doctor later."

But, in the afternoon, there was a knock on the door.

Weetzie answered it without thinking, and there stood the Lanka.

"Tell Max he had better see me or he will get worse," she said.

Before Weetzie could shut the door, she heard My Secret Agent Lover Man say, "Wait."

He had gotten out of bed and was stumbling toward them wearing his trench coat over his pajamas.

"Max," said the woman, "I must talk to you. Tell this girl to let me in. Or I will make her sick, too. I have a Barbie doll that will look a lot like her when I chop off all its hair, and I have plenty of pins to stick into it."

"Weetzie," My Secret Agent Lover Man said, "can I please speak to her? I will tell you everything after."

Weetzie looked at him and at the Lanka and then back at him. He was really sick.

"Whatever you need to do," she said, going into the kitchen.

A little while later, My Secret Agent Lover Man came into the kitchen, too. He looked better, as if the fever had broken. "She's gone.

Now I have something to tell you," he said, sitting down beside her.

"When I went away I was very confused," he began. "I knew I was afraid of having a baby, and I hated myself for being afraid. And I was so jealous of you with Dirk and Duck that I couldn't even think. I just had to leave.

"So while I was away, all I thought of was you. And one day I saw a sign that said 'Jayne Mansfield Fan Club.' The picture of Jayne Mansfield reminded me of how you make that siren noise out of *The Girl Can't Help It*, and I went to the place it said. It was a house in a run-down part of town, real spooky and dark, and there were all these people wearing white wigs and doing drugs and watching weird old Jayne film clips and talking about the sick way she died. How her head got cut off in her pink T-bird or something. I was such a wreck from being without you, and from not eating, and from sleeping in my car, and from drinking too much that I just stayed and watched and listened. And then this one woman, Vixanne Wigg, the one today, she asked me if I needed a place to stay, and I did, so she let me stay in the attic of this house where she lived. But soon I realized that these people were pretty sick. They were witches. They had séances and shit, and some pretty bad things happened."

"Like you saw maggots in the sink, and then they were gone, and someone hanged himself in the backyard, and you started to leave but Vixen or Vixanne or whatever seduced you and you slept together just like in your movie, right, *Max?*" Weetzie said.

My Secret Agent Lover Man looked down at his blue suede creepers, and then he looked into Weetzie's eyes. "That's right," he said. "I was very sick then, Weetzie, and now there is more. I left the next day. We only slept together once. It was a terrible thing. But now she says she is pregnant and she needs money for the abortion, so I gave her money, and now she'll leave us alone. But I had to speak to her because she is very powerful and she could have made you sick, too."

"She could not have made me sick," Weetzie said. "You got sick because you felt guilty and afraid."

She got up and walked out of the room.

When she told Dirk and Duck that night they said, "Miss Weetzie Girl, I bet she did make him sick. But don't be mad. Don't hang on to it. He loves you."

And Weetzie remembered him sweating and shaking and gasping in the night and twisting with pain as if he were a Ken doll stuck with pins, and she knew she couldn't be mad for long, and when he came to her that night and stood there so vulnerable and naked and with painful memories tattooed on his body, she forgot everything except that he was back.

Months passed, and the Jayne Mansfield witches were only a movie, and everything was happy in Fifi's cottage. Until the witch baby appeared on the front step.

Duck came into the house one day, carrying a basket. "Look what I found on the front step," he said.

Inside the basket was a newborn baby with purple, tilty eyes and pouty lips. There were a Ken doll and a Barbie doll with chopped-off hair in the basket, too, and Weetzie took one look at the baby and knew who it was.

"It is the witch baby," she said.

"What?" Dirk and Duck said.

"It is My Secret Agent Lover Man and Vixanne's witch baby," Weetzie said.

My Secret Agent Lover Man sat silently for a moment and then he said, "She lied. I'll find her and give it back. I'm sorry, Weetzie."

The witch baby began to cry.

"She is beautiful," Weetzie said. "Even if her mother is a Lanka witch."

Weetzie took the witch baby out of the basket and held her close until she stopped crying. Cherokee eyed her suspiciously.

Duck said, "What are those?" noticing the Ken and Barbie.

"Those are Vixanne's voodoo dolls," Weetzie said. "I think Vixanne gave them to us as a peace offering."

"Vixanne is evil," My Secret Agent Lover Man said. "I've got to give this baby back."

"If she is evil, we can't do that," Weetzie said. "We have to take care of this baby."

"Yeah, we can call her Witch Baby," Duck said. "How totally cool!"

"No, we can call her Lily," Weetzie said. "And she can be Cherokee's sister. Okay, Cherokee Love?"

Cherokee didn't look pleased. My Secret Agent Lover Man picked her up and put her on his knee and gave her the Ken doll to play with. This made her smile.

"If you can accept Cherokee as yours without being sure, then I can accept Lily, even though I know she's not mine; I can accept her because you are her daddy-o," Weetzie said. "Besides, she is cool and she likes me. What do you guys think about keeping her?"

"I hope she is not a voodoo queen already," Dirk said.

"She is only a baby," Weetzie said.

"I hope she is not going to hex me if I don't give her her favorite kind of Gerber's," Duck said.

"She is only a baby," Weetzie said.

"She is a witch baby," said My Secret Agent Lover Man.

"Look at her," Weetzie said. "She is *your* baby."

My Secret Agent Lover Man looked at Lily's pointy little face.

"What does Cherokee think?"

Cherokee smiled and clapped her hands.

"It is cool with me," said Duck. "It will be like *Bewitched*."

"Me too," said Dirk.

They all looked at My Secret Agent Lover Man.

"Okay," he said. "Witch Baby, I mean, Lily, welcome to the family."

Weetzie put Lily onto his other knee.

It was not easy at first. Witch Baby was a wild witch baby. The name Lily never stuck.

As soon as she could walk, she would run all over the house like a mad cat, playing torpedo games. As soon as she could talk, she would go around chanting, "Beasts, beasts, beasts," over and over again.

"Who taught her that?" Weetzie asked Duck suspiciously.

"I swear, she just knew it," Duck said. "Pretty creepy, huh?"

Once, Witch Baby pulled Cherokee's hair and ran away laughing shrilly. The next night, Cherokee cut off Witch Baby's shaggy black hair with a pair of toenail scissors while the witch baby slept. Witch Baby ate and ate but she stayed as skinny as bones and she became more and more beautiful.

"What are we going to do with her?" My Secret Agent Lover Man said.

"She just needs time and love," Weetzie said. "It must be hard for her, knowing she's a witch baby. Besides, I was a terror when I was little, too."

And so, Witch Baby stayed on in the house, and took turns terrorizing Cherokee and being terrorized by Cherokee, and eating up all of Duck's Fig Newtons, and using Dirk's Aqua Net, and insisting on being in My Secret Agent Lover Man's movies, and dressing up in Weetzie's clothes, and pulling heads off Barbie dolls and sticking them on the TV antenna and ruining the reception.

But that's how witch babies are.

Shangri-L.A.

WEETZIE AND MY SECRET Agent Lover Man and Dirk and Duck and Cherokee and Witch Baby and Slinkster Dog and Go-Go Girl and the puppies Pee Wee, Wee Wee, Teenie Wee, Tiki Tee, and Tee Pee were driving down Hollywood Boulevard on their way to the Tick Tock Tea Room for turkey platters.

"They are already putting up Christmas lights," Duck said.

"It's only the beginning of October," My Secret Agent Lover Man said.

"They're making a movie," Dirk said.

Cherokee clapped her hands for the feathery golden bridges of lights that were being strung from Frederick's of Hollywood to Love's.

"We live in Shangri-la," Weetzie said. "Shangri Los Angeles. It's always Christmas."

"That's it!" My Secret Agent Lover Man said.

"What?" they all asked.

"The name of our new movie."

Shangri-L.A. was a remake of *Lost Horizon*, except that in the movie the horizon was a magical Hollywood where everyone looked like Marilyn, Elvis, James Dean, Charlie Chaplin, Harpo, Bogart, or Garbo, everything was magic castles and star-paved streets and Christmas lights, and no one grew old. Weetzie played a girl on her way to the real Hollywood to become a star. The bus on which she is traveling crashes, and when she regains consciousness she and the other passengers who have survived find themselves in the magic land. Weetzie falls in love with the Charlie Chaplin character from Shangri-L.A., and he tells her she can stay there with him and never grow old. She doesn't believe him and insists that they leave together. They fix the bus and drive away, but he immediately ages and dies, leaving her caught in the real Hollywood.

"Hell-A," My Secret Agent Lover Man said.

Making the movie was like dreaming twenty-four hours a day. Weetzie styled her blonde hair in Marilyn waves, and wore strapless satin dresses and rhinestones. She made fringed baby clothes and feathered headdresses for Cherokee and tutu and gauze wings for Witch Baby. Dirk had grown out his Mohawk into a ducktail, and he wore sparkling suits and bolo ties. Duck, in leather, squinted his face up, pretending to be Jimmy Dean. And

My Secret Agent Lover Man, in a baggy suit, walked toes out, his eyes like charcoal stars. They drove around in the T-bird eating ice cream and filming. In the movie, they got to be a rock band. Dirk and Duck played guitar, My Secret Agent Lover Man bass, Valentine and Raphael drums. Weetzie and Cherokee and Witch Baby and Ping sang. They performed "Ragg Mopp," "Louie-Louie," "Wild Thing," and their own songs like "Lanky Lizard," "Rubber-Chicken Strut," "Irie-Irie," "Witchy Baby," and "Love Warrior."

The movie was going very well except they weren't sure about the ending.

"We should ask your dad," My Secret Agent Lover Man said. "He is great at those things."

"Maybe I'll go visit him," Weetzie said. "He hasn't seen Cherokee in a long time, and besides, I'm worried about him."

So Weetzie and Cherokee went to New York to see Charlie Bat.

Charlie was unshaven and he looked even taller because he was so skinny now. He stood in the doorway of the dark apartment shaking his head.

"My babies," he said.

Being with Charlie was always a romantic date. The first day, he took them to the Metropolitan Museum, where they looked at Greek marbles and French Impressionist paintings and costumes until their eyes were blurry and their feet were sore. Weetzie loved the Egyptian rooms the most.

"They spent their whole lives covering these walls with pictures," Charlie said, showing them gods, goddesses, stars, eyes, rabbits, birds, on the tomb walls. "And they filled the tombs with everything you could want. Now that's the way to die."

After the museum, they went to Chinatown and ate squid and broccoli and hot-and-sour soup. Then they wandered through the angled streets that smelled meaty and peppery. The Chinatown museum looked like a movie set and inside was a dancing chicken—a real, live chicken that turned on its own tunes with its beak and did a slidy dance for seventy-five cents. Charlie Bat made the chicken dance and he played air hockey with Weetzie. Then, on the way home, he bought cannolis in Little Italy for all of them.

The next day, Charlie took them to the top of the Empire State Building, and there was his city spread out in front of them. It reminded Weetzie of the time she and My Secret Agent Lover Man had hiked to the top of the Hollywood sign, and she had dreamed of Cherokee and he had been afraid. She wished that the world could be the way it looked from up here—that Charlie could live in a city of perfect buildings and cars and people if he was going to live so far away. The Chrysler Building looked like an art-deco rocket that had caught fans of stars on its way up, and the Statue of Liberty looked like a creature risen green and magical from the sea, and everything looked at peace in the blue, clear day. Charlie bought Cherokee a bottle filled with tiny buildings and blue glitter and water, and she shook it and laughed, watching the glitter come down, and Weetzie wished she could shake blue glitter around all of them—keeping them sparkling and safe.

By the time they came down in the elevator, they all had blue glitter on their eyelids and cheeks from the little bottle.

Charlie took them out for Italian food and French food and Jewish deli and lobster. He bought them strawberries and whipped cream at the Palm Court in the Plaza Hotel, where musicians played to them among the peachy marble columns, mirrors, and floral tapestry chairs. He took them to galleries and shops in SoHo and the East Village and bought them gifts: flowers, Peter Fox shoes for Weetzie, and a Pink Panther doll from F.A.O. Schwarz for Cherokee. Charlie smiled, but he looked lost.

"Are you okay, Daddy?" Weetzie asked.

They had come to Harlem for breakfast. On the street, a man in a black hat had touched Charlie's shoulder and muttered something about "Doctor Man," and Charlie went pale and started to cough as he walked away. Now they were in Sylvia's, eating eggs and grits and biscuits and sweet-potato pie.

"I'm okay," Charlie said. He was on his third cup of coffee and hadn't touched his breakfast. "How's Brandy-Lynn?"

"She is okay," Weetzie said. "She doesn't like the idea of Cherokee having three dads."

"Well, it is a little hard to get used to," Charlie said.

"I think she really misses you," Weetzie said. "You should come and visit."

"And how is that boyfriend of yours?" Charlie asked, trying to change the subject. "The one with the funny name."

"You mean My Secret Agent Lover Man."

"That sure is a funny name," Charlie said.

Weetzie laughed because Charlie had named her Weetzie and his last name was Bat.

"What is Cherokee's last name?" Charlie asked. "Is it My Secret or Secret Agent or Lover or what?"

"Bat, like ours," Weetzie said. "Cherokee Bat."

"She is a wonder," Charlie said dreamily,

looking at his granddaughter in her pink fringed coat. "Cherokee Bat . . ."

Before she left, Weetzie asked Charlie how to end *Shangri-L.A.*

"Maybe this girl tries to get back by taking drugs," he said. "And she dies."

"That is such a sad ending, Dad," Weetzie said with dismay. She knew something was wrong. The paint on Charlie's apartment walls had cracked and chipped and his eyes were as dark and hollow as the corners of the room.

Charlie sighed.

"Move back," Weetzie said. "It is no good for you here. You could work on the movie. We need you. In L.A. we have a fairy-tale house. We have pancakes at Duke's, and dinners at the Tick Tock Tea Room. We have the sky set; remember, you used to take me to see it, and Marilyn's star. And we have Cherokee."

Charlie said: "Weetzie, I love you and Cherokee and . . . Well, I love you more than everything. But I can't be in that city. Everything's an illusion; that's the whole thing about it—illusion, imitation, a mirage. Pagodas and palaces and skies, blondes and stars. It makes me too sad. It's like having a good dream. You know you are going to wake up."

"Daddy," Weetzie said. "Please come home."

"I love you more than everything," Charlie said. "You and Cherokee and Brandy-Lynn still, too. But I can't come back. It would hurt you."

So Weetzie and Cherokee had to leave New York. They left Charlie Bat standing at the airport in his trench coat. He was smiling, but his eyes were like dark corners.

"Mom," Weetzie said. "I am worried about Charlie."

Brandy-Lynn looked up from polishing her nails. "What is it? What's he doing to himself?"

"I think you should call him," Weetzie said.

"It makes me too sad," said Brandy-Lynn.

Charlie was dreaming of a city where everyone was always young and lit up like a movie, palm trees turned into tropical birds, Marilyn-blonde angels flew through the spotlight rays, the cars were the color of candied mints and filled with lovers making love as they drove down the streets paved with stars that had fallen from the sky. Charlie was dreaming of a giant poppy like a bed. He had taken some pills, and this time he didn't wake up from his dream.

Weetzie and My Secret Agent Lover Man and Dirk and Duck and Cherokee and Witch

Baby huddled on the pink bed and cried. Grief is not something you know if you grow up wearing feathers with a Charlie Chaplin boyfriend, a love-child papoose, a witch baby, a Dirk and a Duck, a Slinkster Dog, and a movie to dance in. You can feel sad and worse when your dad moves to another city, when an old lady dies, or when your boyfriend goes away. But grief is different. Weetzie's heart cringed in her like a dying animal. It was as if someone had stuck a needle full of poison into her heart. She moved like a sleepwalker. She was the girl in the fairy tale sleeping in a prison of thorns and roses.

"Wake up," My Secret Agent Lover Man said, kissing her. But she was suffocated by roses that no one else saw—only their shadows showed on her lips and around her eyes.

"Weetzie," he said, kissing her mouth. "You are my Marilyn. You are my lake full of fishes. You are my sky set, my 'Hollywood in Miniature,' my pink Cadillac, my highway, my martini, the stage for my heart to rock and roll on, the screen where my movies light up," he said.

Weetzie curled up in a little ball in the bed.

"Weetzie," he said, "your dad's dead. But you aren't, baby."

She put her arms around him and cried. Their clothes fell away like clothes in a dream— like a dream peels away when you wake up. Their bodies clung together like warriors fighting out the pain in each other.

My Secret Agent Lover Man finally relaxed, his body becoming heavy with sleep. Weetzie held on to him.

"Don't sleep," she said. "Don't sleep. How can we sleep? Suddenly I felt what it is like to know I am not always going to be able to see you and touch you."

My Secret Agent Lover Man wrapped her in his pale warrior arms. The veins pulsed with blue peace like rivers that lead to a mountain lake. Weetzie shut her eyes finally, and the roses did not grow over her in the night. She dreamed that she and My Secret Agent Lover Man were holding hands and climbing a waterfall.

Weetzie went to see Brandy-Lynn the next day.

Brandy-Lynn was drinking vodka and lying on a chaise lounge by the pool. She wore curlers and she was getting very tan.

"When I was a kid my mother brought me to Hollywood," Brandy-Lynn said. "We lived at the Garden of Allah. She left me alone all day and I went around the pool with my cute little autograph book. It said 'Autographs' on the cover in gold. Clark Gable even signed it! Everyone was so gorgeous. I used to walk to

Schwab's and have a hamburger and a milk-shake for dinner, and I'd swivel around and around on the barstool reading Wonder Woman comics and planning how it would be when I became a star. But what I really wanted was a Charlie Bat. I always loved that man. What happened, Weetzie?"

Weetzie hugged Brandy-Lynn. She felt greasy from the suntan oil and her shoulders felt very small.

"He loved you too, Brandy-Lynn," Weetzie said. "Now that's enough." She took away the bottle of vodka. "Let's go out for some health food."

"Did he really?" Brandy-Lynn said. A blurry lipstick smile showed through her blue-mascara-tinted tears. "I haven't been a very good mother, have I?"

"You are a wonderful mother."

"He was the man of my dreams. . . ."

◎   ◎   ◎

At the end of *Shangri-L.A.*, Weetzie played a scene in which the starlet shoots up so she can get back to the dream city. After she dies of an overdose in her apartment, she is transported back. In the final scene, she is reunited with the Charlie Chaplin bass player, and the band performs "Love Warrior" in a *Casablanca* nightclub filled with fans, fronds, and fireflies. Then darkness.

"This film is dedicated to the memory of Charlie Bat," it said on the screen.

Love Is a
Dangerous Angel

ONE DAY, DUCK CAME HOME crying. Weetzie and My Secret Agent Lover Man and even Dirk had never seen Duck cry before, except when Charlie Bat died. They all sat very still and looked at him. Then Dirk got up from the couch and tried to hug him, but Duck pulled away, ran to the blue bedroom, and shut the door.

"Ducky. Duckling. Rubber Duck," Weetzie called.

Dirk got very quiet and kept knocking on the door.

Cherokee and Witch Baby began to cry

and My Secret Agent Lover Man took them in his arms.

Duck would not come out. They said they were going to Mr. Pizza and then rent *Casablanca* on VHS, but he would not come out. They said they were going surfing in the morning, but he would not come out. Finally, after midnight, Dirk tried the door and found it was unlocked. He got into bed next to Duck and looked at the sweatshirt with the picture of Howdy Doody (Duck wore it backward because, otherwise, he said, it kept him awake), and at the blonde hair and the boxer shorts with ducks on them that he had bought for Duck for Valentine's Day, but he didn't touch Duck. It was as if they were far away from each other and he didn't know why. Dirk watched Howdy Doody rise and fall with each sleep breath until Dirk fell asleep, too.

In the morning, Duck wasn't there. Dirk

jumped out of bed, his pounding heart making him dizzy. He ran outside in his boxers and saw that Duck's bug was not there. He ran back inside and saw a note on the table:

Dear Weetzie, My Secret Agent Lover Man, Cherokee, Witch Baby and my dearest, most darling Dirk,

I found out yesterday that my friend Bam-Bam is sick. He is really sick. The world is too scary right now. Even though we're okay, how can anyone love anyone when you could kill them just by loving them? I love you all too much. I'm going away for a while. I will never forget you. And Dirk, I will always love you more than anyone.

Duck

Dirk grabbed his clothes and keys and ran outside and jumped in Jerry. He drove all over the city that day and Weetzie and My Secret Agent Lover Man called all their friends and the restaurants, bars, and stores where Duck hung out. Valentine and Ping made flyers and had them posted all over the city. But there was no trace of Duck.

Dirk came home the next morning unshaven and with dark circles around his eyes. He had been driving around all night.

"I went to the picnic tables on Zuma Beach where we used to sleep, and I went to Rage and Revolver and Guitar Center and El Coyote and Val Surf, and I called everyone. I went to the hospital where Bam-Bam is. No one knew anything. No one's seen him," Dirk said in a monotone. He collapsed on the couch.

Weetzie made tea and rubbed his back,

and My Secret Agent Lover Man told him Duck would come back soon, that Duck was just facing this for the first time and it would be okay. But Dirk hardly felt Weetzie's hands on his back or heard My Secret Agent Lover Man's words. His muscles felt like water, his eyes were blurry; he felt as if someone had cut him and he was losing blood. He thought of his lover and his best friend and his date—his Major #1 Date-Mate Duck Partner.

You are my blood, he thought.

"I'm going to search for him," Dirk said the next day. "Jerry and I are going to find him."

"But how will you know where to go?" Weetzie asked. "Maybe we should hire someone to help us." But she knew that Dirk had to go. She kissed him and packed bags and picnic baskets and thermoses and

Spiderman lunch pails full of bagels, string cheese, chocolate-chip cookies, milk, apples, and carrot sticks. My Secret Agent Lover Man slipped some cash and a Dionne Warwick tape into Dirk's pockets. They all hugged and kissed, and Cherokee and Witch Baby cried.

"I'll let you know," Dirk said, before driving away in Jerry.

You are my blood, Dirk thought over and over to himself as he drove north on Highway 5 in the startling mirage of heat. Everything was the same for miles—dry and yellow— the earth, the sky. He passed a herd of cattle waiting to be slaughtered. The smell made his stomach grip like a fist. He stopped at McDonald's but kept thinking of the cows and ordered a Filet o' Fish and a milkshake. The tourists stared at his black-dyed hair, his torn Levi's, round sunglasses. Some of the sunburned, blinking faces reminded him of raw meat.

Dirk got back into Jerry and drove some more. He felt as if the road were pulling him along and he followed it—he felt like blood in the road vein. He thought of Duck—seeing the blue eyes full of summer, the tan, freckled shoulders, the surfer legs gilded with blonde hair.

Dirk arrived in San Francisco at night. The lights shone and he smelled the cold, bread baking, gasoline. He drove around the Haight where people all wore leather and ate burritos. In a bar where everything looked blue, he felt like a fish in an aquarium as he watched Billy Idol videos next to a man in a muscle T-shirt. On Polk Street there were fewer men than he remembered from the last time he had been there with Duck—fewer men dressed in chains, less swaggering in the strides of the men. It was quieter on Polk Street. The ice-cream store was crowded.

Where are you, my Duck? Dirk thought, looking at the faces of the men eating ice cream as if it would ease some pain.

Dirk drove to Chinatown and walked around the streets that were already emptying as the restaurants closed and the shop owners brought in the porcelain vases, the parasols, kites, screens, jade, and rose quartz and locked their doors. Flyers for Chinese films flapped in the wind. There were carcasses of birds strung up in the windows. Dirk zipped up his leather jacket and walked with his head down but his eyes kept sight of everything around him, of every person he passed. He moved like a piece of blown paper through the windy, hilly Chinatown streets.

It was very late when Dirk went to

Hamburger Mary's. Everyone looked drunk under the old Coca-Cola signs in the rooms that smelled of meat, onions, and sawdust. Dirk remembered when he had come here with Duck and how they had held hands the whole time they ate their hamburgers, not even worrying, for once, about what people would think. He put money in the jukebox and pressed "Where Did Our Love Go" by the Supremes, but he left Hamburger Mary's before it played.

Dirk crossed the street to the bar called the Stud. The place was packed and steaming; Dirk could hardly breathe. He went and stood close to the bar while everyone pressed in around him—the leathered, studded, mustached men in boots, the little surf boys with LaCoste shirts, Levi's, and Vans, the long-haired European-styled model types in black. Dirk stood there looking around and then his heart began to beat very quickly and then he felt like crying.

Who was that beautiful blonde swaying drunkenly on the edge of the dance floor and smoking a cigarette. Who was that beautiful blonde boy?

Love is a dangerous angel, Dirk thought. Especially nowadays.

It was Duck.

Out of all the bars and all the nights and all the people and all the moments, Dirk had found Duck.

Dirk went up to him and looked into his eyes. Duck dropped his cigarette and his eyes filled with tears. Then he fell against Dirk's shoulders while the lights fanned across the dark dance floor like a neon peacock spreading its tail.

"How did you find me?" Duck asked as Dirk led him out of the Stud.

"I don't know," Dirk said. "But you are in my blood. I can't help it. We can't be anywhere except together."

"I love you so much," Duck said. "I've been so afraid. I've been to all the bars just watching and getting wasted. And I know people are dying everywhere. How can anyone love anyone?"

Dirk put Duck into Jerry and he drove them to the hotel where they had stayed another time they had visited San Francisco. Dirk ran the bath and undressed Duck and helped him into the hot water. He soaped Duck's back and made Duck's hair into Mohawks and Kewpie-doll curlicues with shampoo before he rinsed him off. Then they got under the pressed hotel sheets and held on to each other.

"It's so sick," Duck said. "I nicked myself shaving that last night at home, and I saw my own blood and I thought, How could I live in a world where this exists—where love can become death? Even if the doctor says we're okay, how could we go on watching people die?"

Duck buried his face against Dirk's shoulder and the streetlamp light shone in through the window, lighting up Duck's hair.

Dirk stroked Duck's head. "I don't know. But we've got to be together," he said.

In the morning, Dirk drove Duck home down Highway 5. They sang along with Dionne Warwick. They stopped for all-you-can-eat pea soup at Anderson's Pea Soup. Dirk made plans for when they got home—they would start working on My Secret Agent Lover Man's new movie (called *Baby Jah-Love* and starring Cherokee and Raphael as a brother and sister whose parents have been separated because of racial prejudice but who are reunited by their children in the end); they would take a trip to Mexico and drink tequila and lie in the sun and play with Cherokee and Witch Baby in the water. They would start having jam sessions and write new songs, start training to run the next L.A. Marathon; they'd become more politically active, Dirk said.

Dirk talked and talked, the way Duck usually talked, and Duck was quiet, but he laughed sometimes, sang along to Dionne, and took off his shirt and opened Jerry's windows to get a tan.

When they got home, it was a purple, smoggy L.A. twilight. Weetzie and My Secret Agent Lover Man and Cherokee and Witch Baby and Slinkster Dog and Go-Go Girl and the puppies Pee Wee, Wee Wee, Teenie Wee, Tiki Tee, and Tee Pee were waiting on the front porch drinking lemonade and listening to Iggy

Pop's "Lust for Life" as the sky darkened and the barbecue summer smells filled the air.

Weetzie ran up to them first and flung her arms around Duck and then Dirk. Then all six of them held on to one another in a football huddle and the dogs slunk around their feet.

That night, they all ate linguini and clam sauce that My Secret Agent Lover Man made, and they drank wine and lit the candles.

Weetzie looked around at everyone—she saw Dirk, tired, unshaven, his hair a mess; he hardly ever looked like this. But his eyes shone wet with love. Duck looked older, there were lines in his face she hadn't remembered seeing before, but he leaned against Dirk like a little boy. Weetzie looked at My Secret Agent Lover Man finishing his linguini, sucking it up with his pouty lips. Cherokee was pulling on his sleeve and he leaned over and kissed her and then put her onto his lap to help him finish the last bite of pasta. Witch Baby sat alone, mysterious and beautiful.

Weetzie's heart felt so full with love, so full, as if it could hardly fit in her chest. She knew they were all afraid. But love and disease are both like electricity, Weetzie thought. They are always there—you can't see or smell or hear, touch, or taste them, but you know they are there like a current in the air. We can choose, Weetzie thought, we can choose to plug into the love current instead. And she looked around the table at Dirk and Duck and My Secret Agent Lover Man and Cherokee and Witch Baby—all of them lit up and golden like a wreath of lights.

I don't know about happily ever after . . . but I know about happily, Weetzie Bat thought.

In 1989, Francesca Lia Block's groundbreaking debut novel *Weetzie Bat* was heralded by *The New York Times* as an "ingeniously lyrical narrative" with a "desperately needed [message] in an era of broken bonds." It began a series of five exhilarating Weetzie Bat books—each receiving equal critical acclaim. Combined together for the first time in *Dangerous Angels*, all the Weetzie Bat books explore personal identity and the strength of love.

Block is also the author of *The Hanged Man*, *Girl Goddess #9*, and *I Was a Teenage Fairy*. Although her work has been praised by a decade of literary critics, her fondest rewards are the responses from her readers whose lives have been touched by her stories: "These are the greatest gifts I could receive."